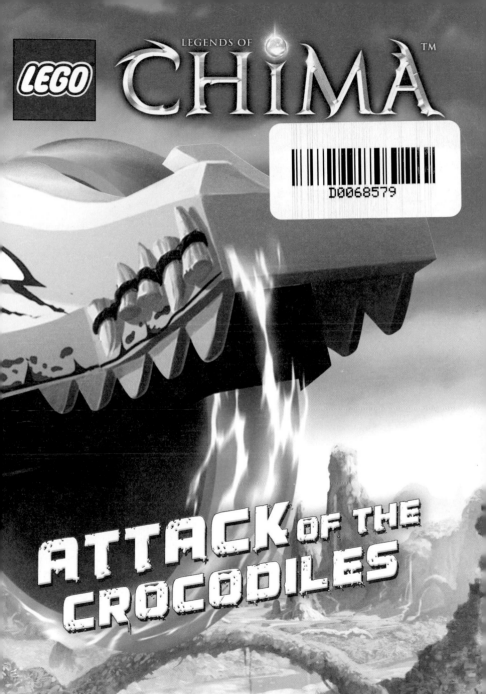

LEGENDS OF CHIMA™

LEGO

ATTACK OF THE CROCODILES

Scholastic Inc.

"Small Packages," "A Simple Bet," and "The Invisible Croc"
written by Greg Farshtey

ISBN 978-0-545-51649-5

12 11 10 9 8 7 6 5 4 3 2 1   13 14 15 16 17 18/0

Printed in the U.S.A.   40
First Scholastic printing, March 2013

TABLE OF CONTENTS

WELCOME TO CHIMA

I am LaGravis, the King of the Lions. We are one of many animal tribes that live here, in the kingdom of Chima.

For many centuries, Chima was a peaceful place. Animals existed side by side in harmony. Then, one day, a bolt of lightning struck the ground and created an earthquake. A giant floating rock called Mount Cavora rose into the sky. Magical waterfalls spilled from Mount Cavora and filled Chima's rivers with a powerful life-force we call CHI. Our ancestors drank the CHI and evolved. They became smarter, more civilized. They built amazing forts and temples, and created advanced machines.

Today, the inhabitants of Chima still rely on CHI, and everything we have created uses its energy.

As the first animals to drink CHI, we Lions are its guardians. It is our greatest duty and highest honor to protect this powerful energy. The CHI is collected in the Lion Temple where it forms into powerful orbs because of special minerals in the Sacred Pool. Once a month we distribute the CHI Orbs fairly to all of Chima's tribes, even those tribes we do not agree with.

Sharing the CHI is necessary for peace and harmony. There can never be too much or too little CHI in the Sacred Pool, or else Chima would fall out of balance and untold catastrophe would befall the kingdom. That's why we Lions must ensure it is regularly used, but never, ever overused.

Each month, there is always one extra-powerful orb of CHI called the Golden CHI. This orb is not given away. Rather, each tribe's finest warriors compete for it in a monthly tournament held in front of the Lion Temple. It is the Lions' responsibility to see that the rules of the competition are followed.

We Lions always act fairly, believe in the rules, and strive to maintain order. For a thousand years no one ever questioned our guardianship of the CHI. Then, one day, a great misunderstanding shook our kingdom. Friends became enemies, and the land of Chima changed forever.

LAVAL

"For the tribes—and for Chima! C'mon . . . It'll be fun!"

Laval is my son and the Lion Prince. One day, he will take my place as the leader of our tribe. Before that happens, though, Laval has a lot to learn about rules and responsibility. He is proud of being a Lion, but for now he is more interested in adventure, fun, and games. I believe in my son, and I know that he will learn it is sometimes necessary to sacrifice your own wants for the greater good.

Laval is also a great warrior. He is skilled with his sword and is an undefeated Speedor racer. But Laval is always a team player, and he hates greed and dishonesty. Laval used to be best friends with Cragger, the Crocodile Prince. Unfortunately, their friendship ended when Cragger changed into a scheming and aggressive rival. Even though the boys are enemies now, Laval hopes that the old friendship can still be restored.

LaGravis says:

Besides greed and lies, there are other things that Laval hates: water, too many rules, and animals who can't take a joke. Which do you think worries me?

CRAGGER

"No mercy. Ever. Really. I mean it."

Cragger is the Crocodile Prince, and the son of King Crominus and Queen Crunket. He has always been an aggressive competitor, living for the rush of victory. Laval actually liked that about him when they first met. Quite soon the two young princes became best friends, sharing countless adventures and the occasional prank. But everything changed when these "pranksters" snuck into the Lion Temple to see the most hallowed place in all of Chima—the Sacred Pool of CHI.

Only animals who have reached the Age of Becoming are allowed to use CHI. The orbs are too powerful for younger animals—it can overwhelm and hurt them. However, despite Laval's desperate attempts to stop Cragger, the Crocodile Prince went against the rules and used CHI. Because of this, a great misunderstanding broke out between the Lions and Crocodiles. A battle ensued, and Cragger's parents were accidently lost in the fight.

Cragger was devastated. He blamed Laval for his parents' death. Now he is determined to lead the Crocodiles against the Lions in battle for control of the CHI.

THE CROCODILES

The Crocodiles have always been a sneaky and slippery bunch. However, when they were ruled by King Crominus, they used to follow the rules of Chima and live in harmony with the other tribes. When King Crominus and Queen Crunket were lost, the young but very ambitious Prince Cragger took the throne.

Incited by his twin sister, Crooler, the new king decided to attack the Lions for control of all the CHI. Little does Cragger know that he is being manipulated by his cunning sister. Crooler is not a strong or skilled warrior, but she is an expert at deceiving others. She uses Cragger to achieve her own goals and enjoys making fun of him behind his back. Under Crooler's bad influence, Cragger has become the fiercest of all the Crocodiles. Even his own tribe members fear him.

The Crocodiles are tough fighters, and even if you're friendly with them, you can never completely trust them. They have allied with the Wolves and the Ravens in the fight against the Lions. Equipped with powerful weapons and battle machines, the three tribes attacked the Lion Temple.

With the help of our friends, the Eagles and the Gorillas, we managed to hold them off. But Cragger hates losing, so we can surely expect a new attack at any time. . . .

"Listen to me, Brother. We'll make the Lions pay."

SMALL PACKAGES

There are many things in this world that can be measured—the length of a day, the number of lions in a pride, the distance from one end of a valley to the other. And then there are those things that cannot be measured, no matter how hard one tries . . . the courage in an animal's heart, the cleverness of his brain, or the daring of his spirit. Only through experience can one learn the true amount of each of these in any living creature.

— King LaGravis

"Muskrats?" exclaimed Laval, the Lion Prince, in disbelief. "Moles? Hedgehogs?"

"Yes," said LaGravis, king of the Lions, to his son. "And beavers and rabbits and mice, as well."

Laval shook his head. "You want me to go talk to all the small creatures in Chima and ask for their *help* in fighting the Crocodiles? You have to be joking, Dad!"

"I'm the king," LaGravis reminded him. "Kings do not joke. Very rarely, we may laugh at something, but only very rarely."

"The Crocodiles and their allies attacked us!" Laval said angrily. "They want control of the CHI that it is our duty to guard and distribute. We need powerful friends among the tribes to help us in this fight, and you're suggesting moles and mice?"

"All of the tribes have their role to play," LaGravis replied. "They may not all be as strong as the Gorillas or soar as high as the Eagles, but that does not mean they have no worth. Laval, as the future leader of the Lion Tribe, I am trusting you to talk with them. Ask if they will be our allies in this fight. Explain that we need their help to defend Chima."

Laval sighed. "Fine, Dad. I'll go talk to them. For Chima."

But later, as Laval went to get his Speedor, he was still frustrated. "What matters now is strength and speed and power," he muttered to himself. "That's all the Crocs understand, and that's what we need in allies."

Laval respected his father more than anyone. But sometimes his dad's thinking was a little . . . old-fashioned. It was great to say that everyone had the same value, big or small. But in a fight, Laval would vote for "big" friends every time.

He climbed aboard his Speedor and raced off into the jungle. There were a lot of mice and moles to find. Speaking to all of them would take all day. Laval grumbled. He had made plans to practice fighting with Eris and Rogon that afternoon. Now he wouldn't be back in time.

As Laval sped deeper into the jungle, he began to calm down. Driving fast always made it easier for him to think. Soon he was zipping through trees and bushes far from the Lion Compound. *It's very quiet out here,* Laval thought to himself. *Too quiet . . .*

Suddenly, four Crocodiles on Speedorz roared out at him from both sides!

"Well, well, what do we have here?" one of the Crocs snarled. "A Lion Prince deep in the jungle with no allies."

Another Croc laughed. "How much CHI do you think a Lion Prince is worth?" he asked.

The first one revved his engine. "Let's take him to King Cragger and find out!"

Laval looked back and forth between the Crocodiles. Escaping was going to be tricky, but it was nothing he couldn't handle. It looked like he would get some practice-fighting in today after all!

"Sorry, mud-lovers," he said as he shot forward. "I've already got plans!"

The Crocs snarled and gunned their engines. "You can't get away from us, Lion!" Soon they were hot on Laval's trail.

Laval raced his Speedor under a low branch, kicking up a cloud of dust as he flew.

"Take that, Swamp Boys!" he cried, shooting around a corner and out of sight.

But the Crocs weren't giving up that easily. The lead Croc motioned to his partners, and they split up to the left and right. When Laval looked back, all he could see was the cloud of dust he had made.

"Now, where did those mud-lovers go?" he said. Just then, one of the Crocs tore out of the bushes and charged at him from the right. Laval whipped his Speedor around. But another Croc was already blocking that path, too. The two other Crocs closed in from the front and back. Laval was boxed in!

"Looks like we've made a Lion-sized trap," the lead Croc laughed.

Laval quickly looked all around him. The Crocs had him cornered . . . but not captured just yet.

"Here's a lesson for you," Laval said with a grin. "When you make a trap, always check it for escape routes first." Gunning his engine, Laval sped toward a flat, angled rock just in front of the lead Croc . . . and zoomed up it like a ramp, right over the Croc's head!

"Woo-hoo!" he cried, zooming off.

The Crocs growled. Now they were really angry. "Get him!" their leader shouted.

They chased Laval farther and farther into the jungle. Soon, the trees and plants began to thin out, and the ground grew dusty. Laval realized he had never taken his Speedor out this far before. And a moment later, he remembered why. Up ahead, stretching as far as they eye could see, was the border of the desert. It was nothing but sand and dust and rocks.

Uh-oh, thought Laval, screeching his Speedor to a halt. *This is very bad.* If he turned back, he would have to fight the four Crocs. But if he went forward into the desert, his vehicle would stop working. Like all Speedorz, the wheel was made from an ancient stone powered by nature. In the barren desert, where no green plants grew, the machine wouldn't last long. Laval would be stranded.

Laval looked behind him. The Crocs were gaining. He knew he was a good fighter, but four-to-one odds were enough to make him think twice. So he revved his engine and headed into the desert.

The vehicle managed to make it only a short distance before it sputtered and died. "I'm a sitting duck out here," Laval said to himself. "I have to hide."

The Lion Prince quickly pushed his Speedor over a large sand dune and out of sight. Luckily, the wind behind him blew fresh sand over his tracks, covering them. Laval peeked over the mound to the edge of the desert.

The Crocodiles had just stopped at the border. They couldn't see Laval hidden behind the sand dune, and their leader was angry.

"*Gna!* Where did that Lion go?" he asked.

The others shook their heads. "Must have headed into the desert, boss."

All four Crocs gulped. They didn't want their Speedorz to die out as well. But they also didn't want the Lion Prince to slip from their claws.

"Maybe we should wait him out," one suggested. "In this heat, he won't last long."

"Or maybe he went back into the jungle?" another said. "I don't see any tracks."

Laval didn't wait to hear any more. He quietly slipped

away, still out of view of the Crocs. His best bet was to try and sneak past his enemies in a little while, when they started to get bored. If they got hungry, they might even head back to the swamp. "I need to find shade," Laval said to himself. "If I'm going to save my strength, I can't let the hot sun get to me."

Laval started walking south. After a while, he became tired and thirsty. He was about to sit down and take a rest when heard a very small voice from below say, "Hey, watch where you're sitting!"

Laval stopped and looked down. There was a little desert mouse waving a tiny fist at him. "You big guys think you can do whatever you want!" said the mouse. "Well, this is my property, right here, not yours."

"This is your property?" Laval asked, surprised. "Where?" Laval looked left and right, but all he could see was sand.

"From that pebble over there," the mouse said, pointing to the north. Then he pointed south. "Then all the way to that sand dune down there."

"I'm sorry. I didn't know," Laval apologized.

"It's okay," said the mouse. "Hey, you're a long way from home, aren't you? There aren't any Lions in the desert."

Laval explained why he was there. "I won't be staying any longer than I have to, but I had better find water pretty soon."

"Stick with me," the mouse said with a smile. "I know all the best places. My name is Alonz, by the way."

Alonz scampered off, with Laval following. After a few minutes, they came to an outcropping of rocks that provided cool shade from the desert sun.

"Thanks," said Laval. "I'll need to stay here a while and wait out the Crocs."

"That might be hard," said Alonz, pointing past Laval. The Lion turned to see that the four Crocs had advanced into the desert and were heading in his direction, though they hadn't spotted him yet.

"Show yourself, Lion!" one of them called. "You can't hide out here forever!"

Laval looked back down at the little mouse. "You'd better find a place to hide," he said to Alonz. "There's going to be a fight, and I don't want you to get hurt. You're too small to stand up to Crocs."

"Ha!" said Alonz. "You don't have to be big to win a fight . . . and sometimes you don't even need to fight to win. Those Crocodiles are in my territory now. I'll show you how to handle them!"

Before Laval could stop him, the mouse darted off toward the Crocodiles. "Wait!" cried Laval. "I'm coming with you!"

"You'll just get in the way," the mouse yelled back cheerfully.

"Stop!" Laval said, using a hand to block the mouse's path. "You can't take on four Crocs by yourself! You're just a mouse!"

"This is my home." Alonz puffed out his chest. "I'm going to defend it. Besides, did you ever stop to think that maybe around here, you're *just* a Lion?"

While Laval was thinking about that, the mouse raced away. When Alonz was about ten feet from the Crocodiles, he started jumping up and down and waving his arms. "Hey, Crocs!" he yelled. "What's big and dumb and smells of swamp? You guys!"

One of the Crocodiles glanced at another. "It's a mouse," he said.

"No kidding," said the other Croc.

"Should I step on him?"

"Nah, just let him squeak. It's good for a laugh."

But the Crocs weren't laughing for long. Alonz ran around them, insulting their looks, their intelligence, and their body odor. After a while, the Crocs started to get annoyed. They chased after him, and Alonz took off as fast as his little legs could carry him.

Alonz was fast, but the Crocs' big legs covered more ground. They were about to catch him! Laval sprang out to help his new friend when, suddenly, the four Crocs sank into the sand up to their waists!

Alonz stopped running. He turned around and laughed. "See, Laval? I told you. They might be bigger and stronger, but they don't know the desert. I do, especially where the patches of soft sand are."

Laval walked up to the four Crocs, chuckling. "Looks like you've been beaten . . . by a mouse."

The Crocs squirmed and glared at Laval. "We'll get you!" they snarled. "As soon as we get out of here."

Laval laughed. "I'd say the only thing you'll get is *waist-deep* in trouble when Cragger finds out about this."

All four Crocs gulped. They had wanted to please Cragger by capturing Laval. But the king wouldn't be happy to hear they'd been defeated by a mouse!

"So, this is what's going to happen," Laval continued. "I'll help you out of that sand before you sink up to your

snouts, and you'll go back to the swamp. In return, I won't tell your king about what happened here today. Deal?"

The Crocs grumbled a lot, but agreed.

With Alonz's help, Laval returned to the edge of the jungle and grabbed a long vine. He brought it back to where the Crocs were still stuck in the sand. Then he tied the vine to one of the rocks and left it within reach of the Crocs. They would be able to use it to pull themselves out of the sand and make their way back to the swamp.

But not before Laval and Alonz were long gone from the desert.

As the Crocs slowly pulled themselves free from the sand, Laval dragged his Speedor back to the edge of the jungle. Alonz went with him, perched on the seat. As soon as they were near the trees and plants, the engine roared to life. Startled, Alonz jumped onto Laval's shoulder.

"Why don't you come home with me?" Laval asked. "We could sure use your help defending the CHI against the Crocs. And I have to say I'm sorry to my dad—he was right about something, and I didn't see it until just now. I think he'd like to meet you."

"Will there be cheese?" asked Alonz.

"Probably," said Laval.

After a minute, Alonz said, "So, what do you have to apologize for?"

"Oh, I had this idea that only small things come in small packages," answered Laval. He smiled. "Turns out I was wrong."

I t was just about Cragger's favorite time of the day: lunchtime! He had asked the cooks to make him an especially good feast today, and he could already smell the food cooking. Best of all, it was all for him. As the king of the Crocodiles, he didn't have to share with anyone.

His sister, Crooler, saw him sitting at the table and came up to him. Crooler was a very sneaky Crocodile, and

she had an idea for a trick to play on Cragger. "You still have a while before the food is ready, don't you?" she asked. "Let's pass the time with a little bet."

"What kind of bet?" asked Cragger.

"Hmmmm," Crooler said. "I bet that you can't swim across the swamp and back in less than five minutes. If you can, then you can have my next ration of CHI."

"I can do that easily," said Cragger, already thinking about how powerful some extra CHI would make him. He dove into the swamp and swam as fast as he could, making it to the far shore and back in record time.

"There!" he exclaimed. "I won!"

"Oh, wait, I forgot," said Crooler. "You have to do half the swim with your eyes closed."

Cragger was annoyed. "You didn't say that was part of the bet," he argued.

Crooler shrugged. "Well, if you don't think you can do it, then we can call it off. . . ." she said.

Cragger shook his head. "You're not getting out of giving me your ration of CHI that easily," he said. He didn't like the change, but he knew he could still win the bet. So he swam across the swamp with his eyes closed, then back with his eyes open.

"Okay, done. I won again," he said, starting to climb out of the swamp.

"Wait, wait," said Crooler. "I'm sorry, there was one more part. You're supposed to dive all the way to the *bottom* halfway across, and then do it again on the way back. And you have to keep your eyes closed the whole time."

Cragger glared at Crooler. He knew his sister hated to lose bets, but this was getting ridiculous. "You can't keep changing the bet just because you lost," he snarled. "I won the CHI and it's mine."

"Of course you did," Crooler said, a soothing tone in her voice. "Just like you will one day beat Laval and the Lions in battle, and control the rest of all the CHI. So don't tell me you're afraid of a little added difficulty in such a simple bet?"

"I'm not afraid of anything!" snapped Cragger. "I'll show you!"

And with that, he dove back into the swamp. He shut his eyes tightly and started to swim through the muddy water.

When he thought he was about halfway across, he dove down deep. Now it didn't matter that his eyes were closed, because it was too dark down here to see anyway. He kept going until his nose struck the bottom, then he swam back up. Once he reached the surface, he made it to the far shore, turned around, and repeated what he had just done on his way back. It was hard, but he still did it in well under five minutes.

This time, he climbed all the way out of the water and stood on the shore. "Done. I won. You lost. Understand? I swam it in under five minutes, and then I swam it with my eyes closed half the way, and then I did it with my eyes closed the whole way and diving to the swamp bottom on both legs of the trip. Now it's time for my lunch!"

Crooler shook her head sadly. "All right, all right. But I don't know how you think you can defeat Laval if you can't even beat your own sister in a bet."

"What are you talking about?" Cragger yelled in disbelief. "I won the bet! W-O-N, won!"

"Well, if you call that winning," Crooler replied. "I mean, that was so easy that Crug could have done it. You left out the part where you were supposed to count to five hundred when you were at the bottom."

Cragger felt like his head was going to explode. "*I* didn't leave that out, *you* left that out! You want me to count to five hundred? Fine! But this is absolutely, positively the last time I am doing this! When I win—and I *will* win—I want your CHI for the next two months, not just one."

Before Crooler could reply, Cragger turned and dove back into the swamp. He repeated the entire routine, including counting to five hundred both ways.

When he was done, he swam to shore and opened his eyes. There was Crooler seated at the table, finishing off his lunch. As he watched, she popped the last morsel in her mouth and smacked her lips. *"Mmmmm,"* she said. "I can see why you were looking forward to this so much!"

"Why, you—you—" sputtered Cragger.

"Oh, and by the way, you were supposed to do all that with one arm tied behind your back," Crooler said, smiling. "So you had better get busy. I'm going to go take a nap. A good meal always makes me sleepy."

Cragger was so angry he could barely speak. But before he could shout back at his sister, she had already walked away to take her nap. Now Cragger would have to wait for the cooks to make *another* meal. And who knew how long that would take?

"Stupid bet," Cragger muttered, sitting down on the shore. Even if Crooler gave him her next two rations of CHI, his stomach was still empty. "Now I'm hungry *and* tired," he grumbled.

Grumble, his empty stomach replied.

THE INVISIBLE CROC

nvisibility—many have sought after this power, believing it would bring them luck, or stealth, or just the ability to do whatever they liked without anyone knowing. But it is often said that what is truly invisible is not that which we can't see, but that which we choose not to see.

— King LaGravis

"I've done it!" cried Cragger the Crocodile. "I've won at last!"

Cragger's two henchmen, Crawley and Crug, were walking behind their king. As soon as they heard what he said, they both started nodding their heads vigorously.

"Oh, absolutely," said Crawley. "No doubt. You are the winner, boss. *Winner.* Everybody else is a loser next to you."

"Right," said Crug. "What he said."

"After today, Laval and his pitiful tribe of Lions won't

be able to stop us from taking all the CHI we want," Cragger continued.

"Wow," said Crawley. "Tell us what you did, boss, so we can feel dumb for not thinking of it ourselves."

Cragger waded into the swamp. The two Crocs followed eagerly behind him. "I made a deal with Rizzo the Raven." Cragger grinned deviously. "It seems Rizzo came across an old alchemist with an invisibility potion. The only one in all of Chima. And I bought it! With this potion, the

Lions won't stand a chance against us. How can they defend their precious CHI against an enemy they can't even see?" Cragger cackled. Crug and Crawley looked at each other, and then cackled along with him.

Cragger rubbed his hands together. "Rizzo is going to deliver it any minute now. And that will be the end . . . gna . . . the end . . ."

Cragger tried to continue speaking, but a little bird had suddenly flown up and started picking at his teeth!

"*Gah!* Plovar, what are you *doing*?" Cragger cried.

The bird tsked. "Craggy-Waggy, did you forget our teeth-cleaning appointment *again*? That's the third time this month!"

Cragger shook his head. "Not now, Plovar. I'm expecting a very important delivery."

But the bird refused to leave. "I'm afraid I must insist," Plovar said. "As I always say, a king's most valuable treasure is his pearly-white smile! Surely Crawley and Crug can accept your important delivery?"

Cragger grunted as the little bird nudged him along to his chambers. "Crug, Crawley, I want you two to guard the potion while I'm getting my teeth cleaned," he said. "Don't let my sister, Crooler, have it!"

"Got it," said Crawley. "Rizzo is going to bring the potion. When it gets here, we should give it to your sister and go get our teeth cleaned."

"Crug," called Cragger, "take care of this."

Crug dunked Crawley's head in the swamp. Crawley came up, spitting swamp water. "Done, boss," said Crug.

Later, the two Crocs were at their posts along the shores of the swamp when Rizzo came into sight. The one-eyed Raven didn't seem to be carrying a bottle of anything. That wasn't good news.

"Hey, boys, is Cragger around?" asked Rizzo.

"He's getting his teeth cleaned," said Crawley.

"Good," said Rizzo. "See, there's been a little, um . . . problem. I got the potion, sure thing, best quality it can be—just don't ask where I got it, right? Anyway, this stuff's so good that the *bottle* turned invisible, too. So don't drop it or you'll never find it, got me?"

Crawley nodded and reached out. Sure enough, he could feel a bottle in Rizzo's claws, but not see one.

Rizzo flew off. The two Crocodiles headed for Cragger's room. Just as they walked in the door, Crawley stumbled and dropped the bottle. They could both hear it rolling across the floor, but of course they could not see it.

"Oh, that's just great," said Crawley. "We had better find it fast!"

They both started searching the floor, holding out their hands hoping to touch the invisible bottle. But before they could find it, they heard Cragger bellow, "Who's there? Is that you, Crawley? Where's my potion?"

"You know what's going to happen when he finds out the bottle is lost?" Crawley whispered.

"Something bad," answered Crug. "What do we do?"

"I don't—wait a minute, I've got an idea," said Crawley. He snatched up an empty bottle from Cragger's shelves and poured swamp berry juice from another jug into it. "See? We'll just tell him this is the potion. When he drinks it and nothing happens, he'll just figure the potion didn't work."

Just then, Cragger stomped into the room with Plovar behind him. The little bird flew off, mumbling something about their appointment being cut short.

When Cragger saw the bottle in Crawley's hand, he brightened up.

"Give it to me!" Cragger exclaimed. He took the bottle and drank it right down. "*Mmmm*. It even tastes good!"

Cragger stood still for a few seconds. Then he smiled broadly, showing his sharp teeth. "It worked! I'm invisible!"

"It did?" said Crug, puzzled because, of course, he could still see Cragger.

"Sure, it did!" Crawley said loudly. He knew better than to disagree with Cragger about anything. "We *can't* see him, can we?"

"Huh? But—" said Crug. Crawley elbowed him in the side. Crug got the message. "I mean, yeah, right . . . can't see a thing."

Cragger's expression turned suspicious. "If you can't see me, why are you two looking right at me?"

"Um, it's your voice, boss," Crawley said quickly. "We're just following your voice. But we can't see you, no, sir."

Cragger's smile returned. "Excellent! First, I have a few surprises for Crooler. Won't my sister be shocked to find out I'm invisible?"

Crawley thought fast. If Cragger went to Crooler, she would be sure to tell him he wasn't invisible.

"Hey, you don't want to do that, boss. Why, if your sister finds out about this, she might get Rizzo to get her a potion, too. You don't want to have an invisible Crooler running around, do you?"

"No!" agreed Cragger. "She's bad enough when you can see her. All right, then . . . I will go straight for Laval. That foolish Lion will never know what hit him!"

Oh, no, thought Crawley. *If he goes and confronts the Lions thinking he's invisible . . . well, Crug and I had better find a good place to hide while he's gone.*

While Crawley was thinking this, Cragger had moved behind Crug. The king picked up a pitcher of swamp water. He snickered and lifted it to pour right on top of Crug's head!

Crug started to turn around to see what Cragger was doing, but Crawley stopped him in time.

"You don't know where he is!" Crawley reminded him in a harsh whisper.

"Sure, I do," Crug whispered back. Then, looking confused, he said, "Don't I?"

"No, you don't. He's invisible!"

"Okay," said Crug. "But does 'invisible' mean everyone can see you?"

"No," whispered Crawley, just as Cragger dumped the pitcher of swamp water all over Crug's head. "It means you think nobody can."

Cragger couldn't wait to get started for the Lions' territory. But Crawley convinced him to wait a little while, just to make sure the potion would "keep working."

That gave Crug time to spread the word. "Boss thinks

he's invisible," he told every Crocodile he came across. "So don't tell him he's not!"

This got Crug a lot of strange looks from some of the younger Crocodiles. But the older ones had been around Crocodile Kings long enough to know you *never* tell them they are wrong.

By midafternoon, Crawley had stalled for as long as he could. Cragger started for the Lion Compound. He smiled as he went, noticing that absolutely no one was paying attention to him.

Suddenly, the sound of running feet behind him made Cragger turn around. Crawley was hurrying down the muddy path, carrying the king's spear. Just before he would have collided with Cragger, Crawley pulled up short and looked all around.

"Boss? Are you here?" Crawley called.

"I'm right in front of you," said Cragger.

Crawley jumped, pretending he was surprised. "Wow! Couldn't see you at all! Hey, you forgot your spear, boss."

"I didn't forget it," Cragger snapped. "My spear wouldn't be invisible. Laval would see it floating in the air and know something was up. Besides, I won't need it to beat him—I'm invisible!"

"Yeah. Right," said Crawley. He was feeling a little sick. It was bad enough Cragger was going to walk right into Laval's hands. But he was going to do it unarmed, too! "Uh, are you sure you don't want to bring your spear? Maybe leave it behind a tree or something when you reach the Lions, you know, in case you need it?"

But one look from Cragger was enough to send Crawley running back to the swamp.

Cragger marched for a long time. He didn't see any other animals—and no one saw him, of that he was very certain.

When he reached the outskirts of the Lion Compound, he saw a guard posted. *This will be fun,* he thought. *I'll march right past that guard and he'll never know it.*

Cragger not only walked right up to the Lion Guard, but he did it while making all kinds of funny faces. At first, the Lion was just shocked to see the king of the Crocodiles heading his way. Then he decided that it must all be a practical joke, because the real Cragger would never do such a thing. One of the other Lions must have disguised himself as a Crocodile.

I'll show him, thought the Lion Guard. *I will completely ignore this fake Cragger.*

And that's just what he did, not even looking in Cragger's direction as the Crocodile went right past him.

He didn't see me! Invisibility is great! thought Cragger. *Now to find Laval.*

For his part, Laval was *not* having a very good day. He had wanted to practice his stalking and fighting skills with his friends in case the Crocodiles ever made trouble. But instead, his father had insisted that he spend the day studying Lion History and traditions. So here he was, sitting on a rock reading an old parchment instead of doing something fun. He was annoyed.

Cragger approached the seated Lion very quietly. He didn't want any noise to give away where he was after all the trouble he had gone to in order to become invisible. But all of the sudden, Laval turned to look in his direction. Instinctively, Cragger darted behind a nearby column.

Cragger smacked his head. *What am I doing?* he thought. *Laval can't see me while I'm invisible. There's no reason to hide.*

"Hello?" called Laval. "Is anyone there?"

Cragger chuckled. *No one that you can see,* he thought to himself. Quietly, Cragger stepped out from behind the column.

But the moment he did, Laval leaped up. "Cragger! What are you doing here?" He reached for his sword.

Impossible, thought Cragger. *He can't see me. It must be a trick!*

Cragger took a few steps to the left. Laval's head turned right along with him.

Maybe it's those Lion Senses of his, Cragger grumbled to himself. *He probably smells me or something. Not sure how; I just bathed three weeks ago!*

Cragger went back to his right. Again, Laval's gaze followed him. Slowly, Laval lowered his sword. "Cragger, what in Chima are you doing?" he asked.

Cragger snarled. "How can you *see* me?" he demanded. "I'm invisible!"

"Huh? No, you're not." Laval shook his head. "You're standing right there."

Cragger muttered under his breath. "When I get my claws on Rizzo . . ." he grumbled. "His potion must have worn off!"

"What potion is that, exactly?" Laval asked.

"The one that made me invisible," answered Cragger. "I've been invisible all day."

"And now you're not," said Laval.

"No," Cragger said, with a shrug. "Apparently not."

"Okay, let's review then," said Laval. "You're the leader of the Crocodiles, and you're surrounded by Lions. You don't have your spear, and you're *not* invisible."

"That's right," said Cragger.

"I think you should run," offered Laval.

Cragger's eyes widened as he suddenly realized just where he was and what was likely to happen next. He took off running back to the swamp as fast as his legs could carry him.

The sun was setting when Cragger finally reached his home. Tired and irritated, he stomped into his chambers . . . and promptly tripped on an invisible bottle! He got to his feet, took a step, and tripped on the bottle again.

Lying on the floor, Cragger looked over at the spot where he had tripped. There was nothing there. Angrily, he reached around and scrapped his claws along the floor feeling for whatever he had stumbled on. But each time he came up empty-handed, only to trip over the invisible object a few minutes later as he was stomping around the room.

Cragger would spend all night trying to find the invisible object. But as he already knew, it's hard to get your claws on something you can't see.